Fifteen Further Funny F

Teacher's Book

Virginia Ferguson and Peter Durkin

Contents

Introduction

Giggle and Grin Books come in three sets: *Fifteen Funny First Books Set 1*, *Fifteen More Funny First Books Set 2*, and *Fifteen Further Funny First Books Set 3*.

Giggle and Grin Books have been designed specifically to enable children with only minimal knowledge of word recognition to begin to read independently. More and more research indicates that learner-readers need simple stories they can read from beginning to end. Such books are generally of an earnest teaching nature – very little humour exists. *Giggle and Grin Books* have been written to fulfil what is considered to be a great need.

No matter what reading approach or program a school has adopted, *Giggle and Grin Books* are intended to supplement it only. In no way are these books designed to be a reading program in themselves. They are intended merely to be an enjoyable adjunct to the school's own reading program.

Giggle and Grin Books will enable children to enjoy their early reading. They will also help children to emphasise specific sounds that they will come across frequently. For example, in *Three Uncooked Pork Chops*, the *or* sound as in *pork* is repeated throughout the story. Similarly, in *Stone Broth*, the *th* sound as in *broth* is used. Words with particular sounds have never been included in the Books simply for the sake of repetition of a sound. The aim has been to produce stories using natural language.

How to Use the Program

The Books
Before you begin, read the story with the children. Each child in the group should have a book if possible.

After Reading the Books But Before Doing the Activities
Do some fun activities after reading the Books. For example, focus on the phonics in the story you have read – but not in isolation. Read the entire story, the entire sentence, the entire word. Play games and have fun based on the stories. Get the children to think of some other words containing the same sounds as those in the story.

The Teacher Books
The activities in the Teacher Books progressively reinforce sounds, beginning with simple vowel sounds and ending with more difficult patterns, such as the letter *o* sounding as *u* in *mother, brother, other.*

Black Line Masters
The black line masters in the Teacher Books are intended to stimulate learning; they are not just time-fillers. They are designed for use by children at varying stages of development, which is why there are frequent instructions for children to go over the page. These activities, to be completed over the page, are to prompt 'the sky is the limit' activities, such as –
- brainstorming
- word development
- writing and drawing.

It is desirable before children begin working on one of the activities that they have read the related story or had the story read to them. The black line masters could be used with groups of five to ten children, each child with his or her own copy of the relevant Book. Activities should then be rehearsed on the blackboard. Although the black line masters are designed for ease of administration by the teacher and independent work by the children, follow-up work is essential. So after completion of each activity, it should be discussed with the children.

Each unit consists of four pages, which are as follows:

The First Page – Word and Sound Recognition Page
The first page usually consists of word recognition and sound reinforcement activities. In every case, children are encouraged to go beyond the page and build their own word lists, and practise sounds and sentences of their own.

The Second Page – Read, Write and Draw Page

The second page always consists of: a wordshapes section in which children are encouraged to examine the words and sounds in the text; a read and draw or a word-building section; and simple reading and comprehension practice. Again, the children, especially fast finishers, are encouraged to go beyond the page to complete their own activities related to the text.

The Third Page – Cloze Page

The third page always consists of a cloze activity. This enables children to revise what they have read and understood, and for the teacher to evaluate children's progress. A self-assessment key is built into these activities.

It is essential that time is spent with the children discussing the cloze activities before any written work takes place. At the earliest levels, the whole activity may be done orally with the children as a group. Teachers should use their discretion as to whether or not the missing words are written on the board so that children can copy them into the correct spaces. In later levels, this will be unnecessary. Older children should be able to rely solely on the text for clues about the missing word or word-part.

The cloze activities focus exclusively on the particular sound that is emphasised in the Book. There is, however, no reason why the teacher could not blank out more words on the cloze page to make it more demanding for better readers.

The Fourth Page – Creative Activity Page

The fourth page consists of a creative activity based on the story in the Book. Activities include: mazes, making models, enlarging pictures, writing and sketching alternative conclusions for the stories, cutting out scenes and arranging them in order, matching words and sentences, and writing and drawing responses to questions.

Three Uncooked Pork Chops

story   storm   pork   airport   corn   short   corner   word   thorn   cork   torn   for

or Word and Sound Recognition Page

Join the sentence to the correct picture.

Tell me a story, Dad.

The storm was wild and windy.

I like pork chops.

The jet landed at the airport.

The ears of corn grow in the paddock.

The short boy has big feet.

The girl is peeping around the corner.

This is the story of *The Three Pigs*.

On the other side

Write as many *or* words as you can. Write a sentence that has a word with *or* in it, as in p**or**k.

or Read, Write and Draw Page

Wordshapes

record	corn	important	north	or	airport

Complete the word families.

m <u>ore</u>
b _____
sh _____
ad _____
_____

c <u>orn</u>
b _____
ac _____
t _____
_____

p <u>ork</u>
c _____
st _____
_____
_____

Circle the correct word.

corn
• John has thorn the page.
torn

fork
• I love roast pork and crackle.
torn

port
• The ship pulled into the storm.
cork

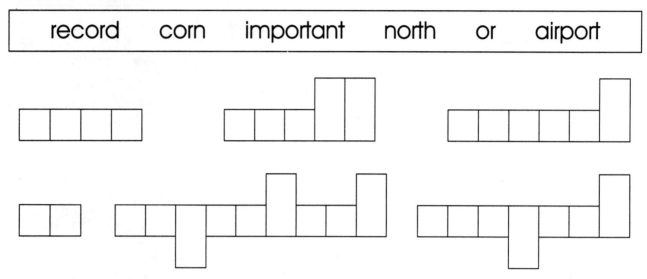

On the other side

Write and draw a story about a stormy night.

or Cloze Page

"Be off with you all!" said Mother Pig.
"The three of you are far too big!
It's imp__ __tant f__ __ you to have homes of your own
— So off you go and leave me alone!
Pack your bags; be on your way.
But listen now to what I say:
The wolf is lurking — watch the beast.
Uncooked _____ chops are his best feast!"
Down the road came a man with straw.
"Pig One, what are you waiting ____?"
Asked Pigs Two and Three as they watched him go
To build his straw house, his heart sinking low.
Along came the wolf.
"Let me in! Let me in!"

"Not by the hair of my chinny chin chin!"

"Then I'll huff and I'll puff
and your house will fall in!"
And it did.
Pig One t__ __e to the house of Pig Two.
"The wolf's on his way! What will we do?"

"If the st__ __ __y's the same, he'll try his old tricks.
He'll huff and he'll puff
And he'll knock down these sticks!"

My score—

Colour in all the *or* words.

or Creative Activity Page

Two-way Puzzle

Fill in the missing letters. Use the Word Bank to help. If you get every word right, the two mystery words in black squares should be clear.

Word Bank

after	chinny	laughter	puff	three
bricks	enormous	pork	straw	

Clues

1 His breathing became an _____ roar.
2 Three uncooked p____ chops.
3 How many little pigs are there? _____
4 "Not by the hairs of our _____ chin chins."
5 They all lived happily ever _____.
6 The first pig's house was made of _____.
7 "I'll huff and I'll _____."
8 The third pig's house was made of _____.
9 "… with happy songs and more and more _____."

The two mystery words are: M_____ P___.

A Rotten Surprise

mice

drive

bike

Smile

Knife

wives

surprise

white

Five

wide

price

tide

i-e Word and Sound Recognition Page

Join the word to the correct picture.

mice			five
bike			wide
knife			smile
white	FOR HIRE	5	drive

Complete the word families.

f<u>ive</u>	m<u>ice</u>	ins<u>ide</u>
al__v__	pr _____	outs _____
h__v__	tw _____	s _____
w__v__ s	n _____	t _____
l__v__ s	_____	h _____

On the other side

Write as many i-e words as you can. Write a sentence that has a word with i-e in it, as in m*i*ce.

i-e Read, Write and Draw Page

Wordshapes

| surprise | five | write | outside | tired | decided |

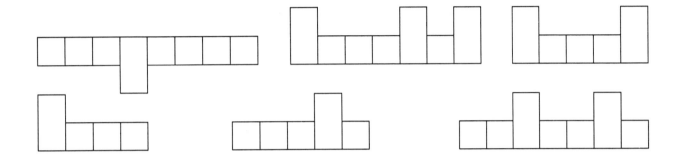

Read and Draw

Five bikes upside down.	Nine tired mice inside a bucket.

Yes or No

- Is your teacher tired? _____
- Would you like a surprise? _____
- Is outside better than inside? _____
- Does 5 + 9 = 16? _____

On the other side

Write and draw a story about a nice surprise.

i-e Cloze Page

Once upon a _ _ _ _ _
there lived a poor farmer
and his _ _ _ _ _.
They were so poor that soon
they had nothing left to eat or drink.
Not a drop!
Not a crumb!
"I'm _ _ _ _ _ _ of this _ _ _ _ _,"
they both sighed.
So one day the farmer's _ _ _ _ _ said,
"There is nothing for it!
We will have to sell Buttercup."
The next _ _ _ _ _ day, the farmer set
out to sell the cow.
On he walked, feeling tired and sad.
Along came a girl
with a small, white horse.

My score—

Colour in all the *i-e* words.

i-e Creative Activity Page

Cut out the pictures, and put them in the correct order.
Paste them on a clean sheet of paper.

Always Room for One More

roof

room

spoon

moon

zoom

loom

hoot

broom

boot   balloon   hoop   kangaroo

oo Word and Sound Recognition Page

Join the words to the correct picture.

- the roof on the house

- the spoon but no dish

- the moon and the stars

- the big boot

- the floating balloon

- the bouncing kangaroo

- put me in the zoo

- dance the hula hoop

Complete the word families.

m <u>oo</u>n	h <u>oo</u>t	br <u>oo</u>m
sp _____	t _____	b _____
s _____	sh _____	r _____
n _____	r _____	l _____
sw _____	l _____	z _____

On the other side

Write as many oo words as you can. Write a sentence that has a word with oo in it, as in room.

Always Room for One More

 oo **Read, Write and Draw Page**

Wordshapes

room	kangaroo	hoot	balloon	broom	spoon

Read and Draw

The man in the moon.	A zoo in a school.

Circle the correct word.

soon
• The dish ran away with the spoonful.
spoon

moon
• The man in the mood laughed out loud.
moody

On the other side

Write and draw a story about a favourite house or place where you like to stay.

18

oo Cloze Page

Once upon a time,
an old man lived in a little house
with just two _____ —
a bed_____ and a kitchen.
"Moo! ____! Moo!"
There was a cow at the door.
"May I come in?"

"Yes, of course.
There's always _____ for one more."
Toot! _____! Toot!
There was a car at the door.
Seven sailors jumped out.
"May we come in?"

"Yes, of course.
There's always _____ for one more."

My score—

Colour in all the oo words.

oo Creative Activity Page

Draw all the people in the old man's house.

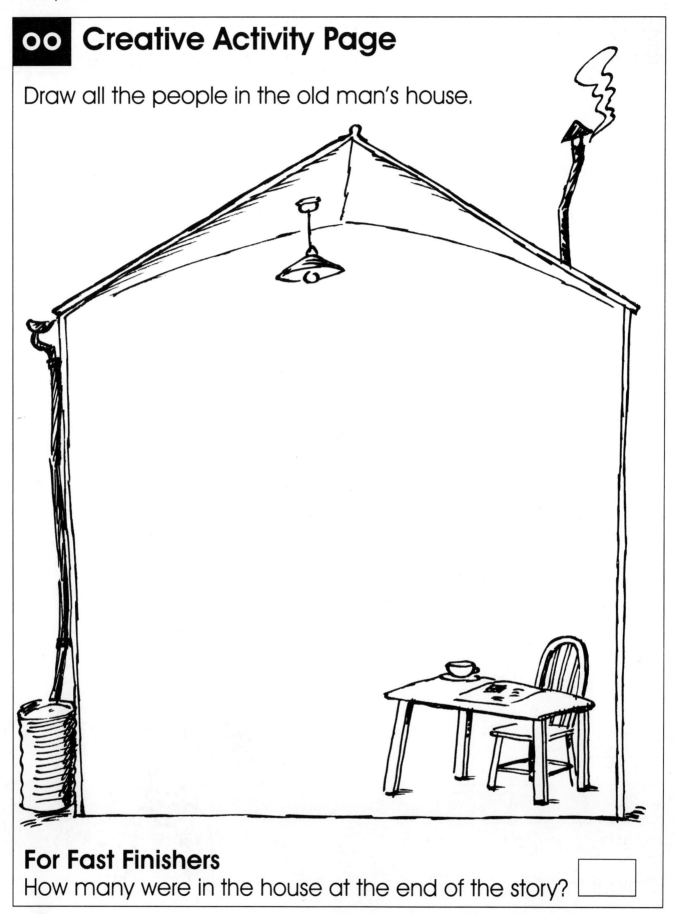

For Fast Finishers

How many were in the house at the end of the story?

No Cooking!

cooking leaping jumping ending plopping thumping

cleaning popping sweeping flying hiding twisting

ing Word and Sound Recognition Page

Join the word to the correct picture.

cooking		cleaning
hiding		popping
leaping		sweeping
twisting		flying

Complete the word families.

h<u>opping</u>	j<u>umping</u>	<u>ending</u>
st _____	d _____	bl _____
p _____	l _____	m _____
l _____	th _____	t _____
pl _____	p _____	s _____
_____	_____	_____

On the other side

Write as many *ing* words as you can. Write a sentence that has a word with *ing* in it, as in cook*ing*.

ing Read, Write and Draw Page

Wordshapes

stirring bubbling flinging bouncing hiding vacuuming

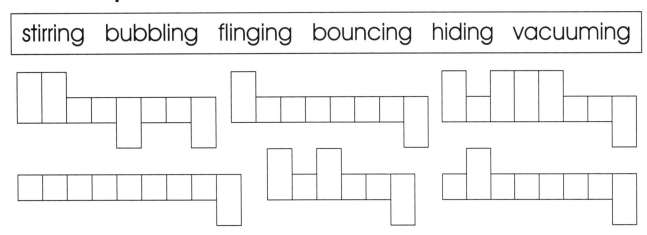

Read and Draw

An overflowing bath dribbling over everything.

Yes or No
- Are cats often barking? _____
- Are children always helping? _____
- Are teachers never shouting? _____
- Are tigers sometimes growling? _____

On the other side

Write and draw a story about the children getting into mischief while Mum and Dad are away. What happens when Mum and Dad come home?

ing Cloze Page

Once there were two very naughty children.
Their names were Jessie and Fred.
They couldn't wait for their parents
to go out so that they could get into mischief.
BIG MISCHIEF!
One day their parents said,
"Jessie! Fred! We're _____ out.
No mischief
and ABSOLUTELY no cooking!"
"Who, us?" said Jessie and Fred,
"_____? No way!"
But Fred and Jessie were naughty children,
very naughty children.
First they made STICKY TOFFEE.
plopp____, hissing, stirring,
splurt____, bubbling, catch____
burning, smelling, seep____.
They ate it in the dining room.

My score—

Colour in all the *ing* words.

ing Creative Activity Page

Help Jacques and Karl find their way through the twisting, twirling spaghetti to the big packet of Spiffing Cleaner.

Caps for Sale!

cake

place

chase

sale

space   wave   brace

plane   snake   table   take   lace

a-e Word and Sound Recognition Page

Join the words to the correct picture.

- a birthday cake

- a jumbo jet plane

- a wriggling snake

- a smiling face

- stars and space

- time to wake

- chasing the cat

- tea on the table

Complete the word families.

r__ace__	w__ave__	b__ake__
br _____	br _____	m _____
l _____	c _____	t _____
p _____	w _____	l _____
_____	_____	_____

On the other side

Write as many *a-e* words as you can. Write a sentence that has a word with *a-e* in it, as in c*a*k*e*.

a-e Read, Write and Draw Page

Wordshapes

| made   safer   change   grade   stranger   chase |

Read and Draw

A brave astronaut in outer space.

Yes or No
- Do caps go on the top of heads? _____
- Are trees good places for beds? _____
- Can monkeys and apes talk? _____
- Can monkeys and apes chatter? _____

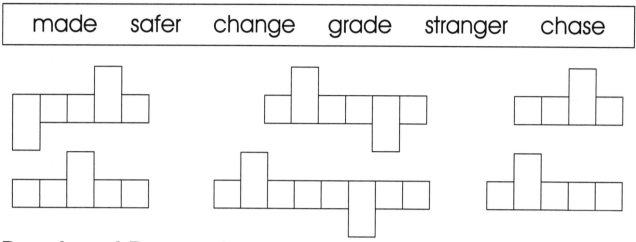

On the other side

Write and draw a story about a tree full of monkeys getting into trouble.

a-e Cloze Page

This is a tale about a pedlar who sold caps.
He would walk from place to _____,
calling, "CAPS FOR SALE! CAPS FOR _____!"
First he put on his old black cap,
then on top of this he placed the
red caps, the green caps, the yellow caps and
finally the blue caps.
… … … … …
One day the old pedlar decided to _____ a nap.
He _____ a bed under a tree
and fell asleep.
"_____ up! You're _____!"
he said to himself.
But, sad to say, his caps had gone.
Only the black one was left.
The red, green, yellow and blue
ones had vanished!

My score—

Colour in all the a-e sounds.

Q. That is the name you go by here—but is not your real name "William Brodie?
A. My Lords, I stand here and claim the protection of the laws of this country, which require two witnesses, on oath, to prove me William Brodie.

You shall have the protection of the laws of this country, but they do not require two oaths to identify you; it requires that the magistrates shall be satisfied you are the same man.

Mr. Groves—I beg leave he may be asked, if he is not a native of Edinburgh?

Question put—the answer, I have been at Edinburgh.

Mr Groves—Is he a Deacon of Edinburgh?

A. I claim the protection of the laws.

Mr Groves—Does he know Mr William Walker, Attorney at law, of the Adelphi, London? *A.* I know such a man.

Mr Groves—Then that William Walker procured the escape of this William Brodie from London, which I can prove by extracts of letters now in my pocket, the originals of which are here in the hands of your officers. I can swear to Mr Walker's writing.

Prisoner ordered to withdraw.

Here the Magistrates asked me if I was ready to swear that, from the pointed description of him and all said circumstances, he was, to the best of my belief, the man required to be given up?—I told them I was.

Mr Duncan was then asked if, from what he knew and what he had heard, he would swear he had no doubt, and believed him to be the man.

Mr Duncan's reply.—I am only a visitor here; and being called on such an occasion, it might, in my own country where I am a Magistrate, have the appearance of forwardness if I was to swear. I am a man of honour and a gentleman, and my word ought to be taken. I do believe, ana I have no doubt, that he is the same man; but I decline to swear it; I'll take no oath.

The Magistrates expostulated, but unsuccessfully, on the absurd idea of saying, "I have no manner of doubt, and verily believe," and refusing to swear, "I

have no manner of doubt!" &c.

As I had previously drawn up an information for Mr Duncan and myself to that effect, he was asked if he would sign it without swearjng?—when Mr Duncan said he would.

The Magistrates then said that they should pay the same compliment to me they did to Mr Duncan, and take my signature to the certificate, without an oath, even to my belief.—Certificate signed.

The prisoner was then ordered in, and the certificate read to him, and asked, If he had not a father?—he replied,—None.

But you had a father, said the Judge—was not his name Brodie?

To this Mr Brodie replied,—" There are more Brodiesthan one."

Then by that, said the Judge, you confess your name is Brodie?

A.—A *lapsus linguae,* my Lord.

Brodie again insisted upon the oaths; but the Judge told him that all they wanted was to be satisfied, which they were from what Mr Duncan and Mr Groves had signed, and partly from a confession of his own.

He was told he should set off as that day; and it was settled at four in the afternoon.

The Judge told me I should have a guide, who would procure the means of conveyance, Ac. I took my leave of them with thanks, &c.; waited on Mr Rich; at four was sent for to the Stadtfaouse, where there was a prodigious crowd; two carriages and four guides, with four horses in each carriage; and the prisoner, being properly secured, we put him into one, and got to Helvoet without much interruption next day at one o'clock packet sailed at five.

N.B. I had wrote a letter to Sir James Harris on the Saturday, requesting the packet to be detained, who informed me by Mr. Rich, with whom I dined on the Monday, that it should be detained to the last moment.

Brodie was watched two hours alternately on board by the ship's crew; his hands and arms confined, and his meat cut for him, Ac.

On Thursday night, eleven o'clock, we arrived at Harwich— supped—set

off immediately, and arrived next day at noon at Sir Sampson Wright's, before whom, and Mr Langlands, Brodie confessed he was the person advertised.

APPENDIX XIII.

Cofies Of Two Autograph Letters Of Deacon Brodie, Hitherto Unpublished.

From Dr. David Laing's MSS. in the University Library, Edinburgh.

I.

To the Right Hon. Henry Dundas (Viscount Melville). Right Honble. Sir

You are no doubt acquainted with my misfortunes. Extracts of the proceedings against me are sent to London by my friends to endeavour to procure a Remission or an Alteration

Facsimile of Deacon Brodie's Letter to the Duchess of Buccleuch. (From the original in Dr. David Laing's collection of,M.S. in the Edinburgh University Library.) of my Sentence. But 1 believe little respect is paid to such Aplications unless supported by respectable Personages. With which view I now most humbly Beseech your interposition and interest in support of this aplioation making at London in my behalf and if possible prevent me from suffering an Ignominious Death to the disgrace of my numerous oonections, even if it were to end my days at Bottony Bay.

I have wrote more fully upon this subject to His Grace the Duke of Buccleugh.

As the time appointed for my Disolution aproaches fast, I most earnestly intreat no time may be lost in writing to London in my behalf.

I now most humbly Beg that you will pardon this Presumption in one of the most unfortunate of the Human Race and whatever may be the result of this Aplication, I shall ever pray for your welfare and hapiness.

I am with the greatest respect Right Honble Sir
Your most obdt and huble Sert
but most unfortunate
Will: Bbodii.
Edinr Tolbooth 10th Sepr 1788 II.
To Her Grace The Duchess of Buccleuch.

Caps for Sale!

a-e Creative Activity Page

Colour the pedlar's caps.

Colour in the ape. Cut around lines. Fold along the dotted lines.

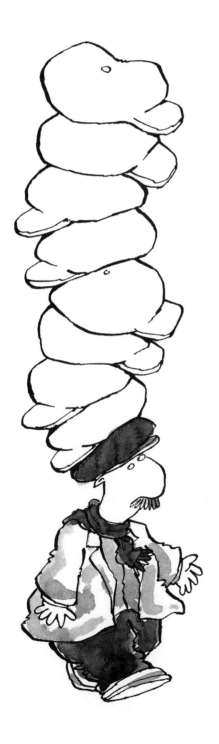

Five Foolish Farmers

mark

park

cart

charm

party

alarm

dart

farm

star

barking

shark

card

ar Word and Sound Recognition Page

Join the word to the correct picture.

cart		farm
party		star
dart		card
shark		barking

Complete the word families.

m <u>ark</u>	<u>art</u>	<u>arm</u>
p _____	t _____	h _____
sh _____	st _____	ch _____
l _____	d _____	al _____
st _____	c _____	
_____	_____	_____

On the other side

Write as many *ar* words as you can. Write a sentence that has a word with *ar* in it, as in f*ar*mer.

Read, Write and Draw Page

Wordshapes

| smart | darling | partners | starve | far | carve |

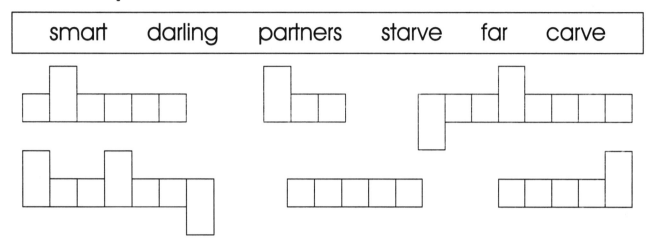

Read and Draw

A Martian at a party.	A prince taking some jam tarts.

Yes or No
• Does a farmer work in the city? _____
• Is a yarn a kind of a story? _____
• Do Martians live next door? _____
• Are foolish farmers smart? _____

On the other side
Write and draw a story about party time at Old MacDonald's Farm.

Five Foolish Farmers

ar Cloze Page

This is a yarn about
five foolish f_____ —
Bluey, Curly, Bart, Shorty and Fred.
"Shake a leg, mates!" called Bart.
"Let's jump on the c____ and head for
Nar Nar Goon where they are having
a p_____ for smart f_____!"
"Just a moment, B___t", cried Bluey,
Curly, Shorty and Fred.
"Let's count ourselves to make sure that
no one has been left behind."
"I'll count," said Curly.
"One, two, three, four.
See, I knew we'd leave someone behind.
There should be five _____ers,
not four — of that I'm sure."

My score—

Colour in all the *ar* words.

ar Creative Activity Page

On a bigger sheet of paper, draw five paddocks. Label them Bluey, Curly, Bart, Shorty and Fred. Cut out the things on this page and stick them in the right paddock.

- Bluey owns the cows and the ducks.
- Curly owns the sheep and the lambs.
- Bart owns the bags of wheat and the pigs.
- Shorty owns the ladder and the horses.
- Fred owns the rabbits and the rakes.

Lies! The Nose That Grew

grew   newspaper   chew   Knew   brew   few

blew   pew   screw   flew   drew   threw

ew Word and Sound Recognition Page

Join the sentence to the correct picture.

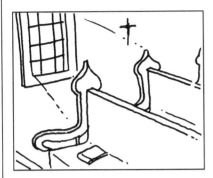

- He blew bubbles into the air.

- The boy's nose grew longer.

- A pew is a seat in a church.

- Have you read the newspaper today?

- You must screw the seat on properly.

- When the rain came, the flower grew.

- The bird flew high in the sky.

- Can the dog chew that big bone?

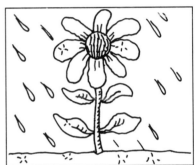

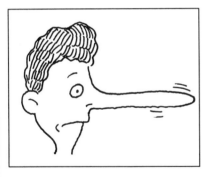

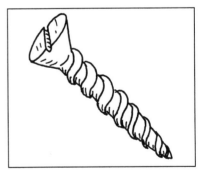

On the other side

Write as many *ew* words as you can. Write a sentence that has a word with *ew* in it, as in *flew*.

ew Read, Write and Draw Page

Wordshapes

| brew | news | newspaper | threw | screwdriver | few |

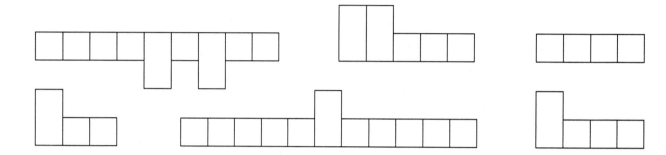

Complete the word families.

g <u>rew</u>
sc _____
dr _____
br _____
_____

n <u>ew</u>
p _____
d _____
kn _____
_____

Join two words to make one bigger word.

• screw + driver = _____

• news + paper = _____

Circle the correct word.

few
• Only a new children could come.
two

flew
• I think Jenny grow 5 centimetres this year.
grew

On the other side

Write and draw a story about when you were caught telling a lie.

ew Cloze Page

"Mum, I need a cake to ch___.
I'm sick of eating stale old st___!"
Said naughty Bill one sunny day
Before he ran outside to play.
Said Mrs Cook, "What can I br___?
Perhaps I'll try something n___.
Now let me see … what can I make?
I think I'll bake a chocolate cake!"
She found a brand ____ recipe
For a chewy, yummy chocolate cake.
She cooked it, iced it, "That's great!"
And then she put it on a plate.
The cake was lovely — dark and rich,
enough to make your tonsils itch.
In fl___ Bill, he saw the plate,
He licked his lips, he couldn't wait.

My score—

Colour in all the *ew* words.

Creative Activity Page

Join each name in the box to the right nose. Use a different colour for each name. Then, finish off the heads of each animal or person.

Billy	crocodile	hippopotamus	pelican	platypus
clown	elephant	kangaroo	pig	teddy bear

Porridge All Over the Place

brother

this

lather

gather

mother

then

them

that

another

there

rather

th Word and Sound Recognition Page

brother	mother	lather	bather	gather	father

_____   _____   _____

_____   _____   _____

Circle the correct word.

       this
- Can we go to then pictures?
       the

          them
- We will go swimming and there we will eat lunch.
        then

     other
- It is over there.
      they

    there
- Can them come too?
    they

      another
- Is there other icecream for me?
    rather

On the other side

Write as many *th* words as you can. Write a sentence that has a word with *th* in it, as in mo*th*er.

th | Read, Write and Draw Page

Wordshapes

another	there	that	rather	this	the

Read and Draw

Mother, father, sister and brother bathing in the sea during the holidays.

Yes or No

- Are brothers bothersome? _____
- Are mothers girls? _____
- Is the word 'the' used often in sentences? _____

On the other side

Write and draw a story about you eating your favourite breakfast.

th | Cloze Page

There once was a poor but
good little girl who lived
alone with her mo__ __er.
One day __ __ey ran out of food
and __ __ere was nothing left to eat.
"I'm starving," said __ __ __ little girl.
"I wish we had an__ __ __ __ __ __ crust."
And her wish came true.
Right __ __ __ __ __ __ in front of her
stood a wrinkled old woman
holding an iron pot.
"Whenever you are hungry,"
said __ __ __ old woman,
"you say, 'Cook little pot!'
and it will cook you some porridge."

My score—

Colour in all the *th* words.

th Creative Activity Page

Cut out the words and pictures. Match them up. Stick them onto a separate piece of paper.

An old woman gave the girl and her mother a magic porridge pot.

The mother couldn't stop the pot. It bubbled everywhere.

There was porridge all over the place.
The little girl rowed home in a boat.

The little girl stopped the pot.
There was such a mess!

Grow Up, Belinda

arrow

crow

burrow

window

sow

grow

pillow

yellow

snow

mowing

know

row

OW Word and Sound Recognition Page

Join the sentence to the correct picture.

- The arrow hit the target.

- The rabbit ran into the burrow.

- Sow the seed in the paddock.

- The pillow is soft and fluffy.

- The snow fell on the snowman.

- Dad is mowing the lawn.

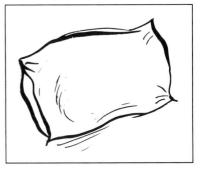

- The crow perched on the roof.

- Open the window wide.

On the other side

Write as many *ow* words as you can. Write a sentence that has a word with *ow* in it, as in *grow*.

47

OW **Read, Write and Draw Page**

Wordshapes

| arrow | wheelbarrow | row | window | sparrow | grow |

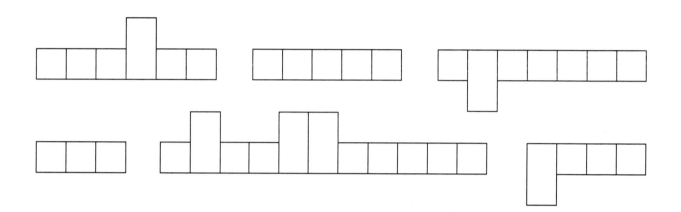

Complete the word families.

b <u>low</u>	r<u>ow</u>	<u>ow</u>
f _____	g _____	s _____
g _____	ar _____	kn _____
pil _____	nar _____	m _____
_____	_____	_____

Yes or No

- A daffodil can be yellow. _____
- A bow goes with an arrow. _____
- Windows can be shut. _____
- Trees need water to help them grow. _____
- A bow tie is worn below your knee. _____

On the other side

Draw and write about a secret you had when you were little.

ow Cloze Page

That night, Belinda collected some
pumpkin seeds, put them under
her pill__ __ and went to sleep.
During the night she began to
gr__ __ a little more.
The next day, just after it had rained,
Belinda s__ __ __ __ed her pumpkin seeds.
They began to __ __ __ __ __ ...
and __ __ __ __ __ ... and __ __ __ __ __.
Soon there were huge pumpkins all
over the garden.
Belinda made
pumpkin toffee
and pumpkin cheesecake
and pumpkin hamburgers
and pumpkin spaghetti
and pumpkin ice cream.

My score—

Colour in all the *ow* words.

© Virginia Ferguson and Peter Durkin 1996. Macmillan Education Australia Pty Ltd.

Creative Activity Page

Help Belinda to grow. Copy the picture onto the bigger squares.

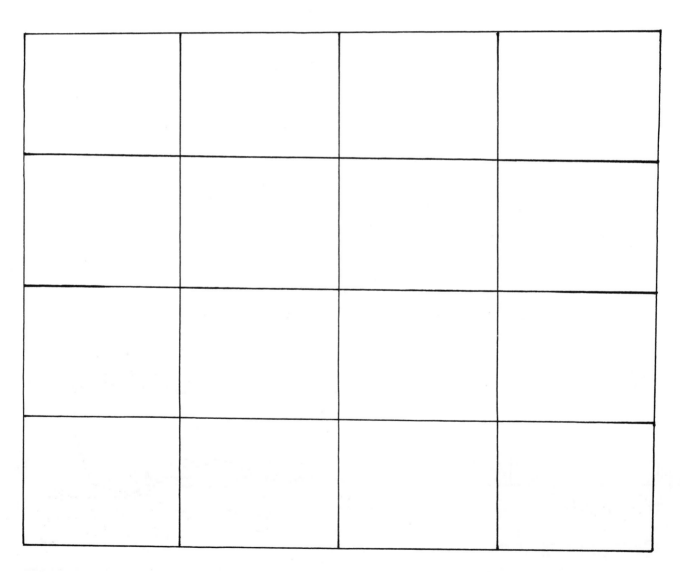

Stone Broth

moth

broth

thistle

healthy

bath

thief

thunder

thumb

path

thimble

teeth

thirteen

th | Word and Sound Recognition Page

Join the sentence to the correct picture.

- The moth flies toward the light.

- A thistle will prickle if you touch it.

- The bath is overflowing.

- Hear the thunder, see the lightning.

- The thimble is on the thumb.

- Vegetable broth makes you healthy.

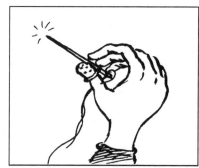

- The thief stole the jewels.

- The path was long and winding.

On the other side

Write as many *th* words as you can. Write a sentence that has a word with *th* in it, as in bro*th*.

th Read, Write and Draw Page

Wordshapes

thimble	three	teeth	thunder	myth	thump

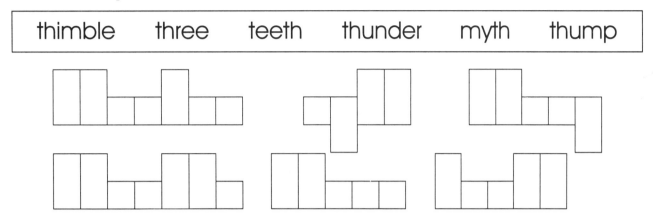

Read and Draw

Thirteen tiny thimbles on thirteen tiny thumbs.	Terrible teeth in a thunderous giant.

Complete the word family.

m oth
br _____
cl _____
sl _____
_____

Yes or No
- Moths can fly. _____
- A thief is good. _____
- You have one thumb. _____
- A thrush is a bird. _____
- Broth tastes sweet. _____

On the other side

Write and draw a story about three moths who wanted to be butterflies.

th Cloze Page

Once a swagman was walking
along a bush path,
when suddenly some__ing tripped him up.
"Thunderation!" he grumbled.
He looked down and saw a __ick,
round stone in the middle of the path.
He picked it up and put it in his pocket.
Soon after, he saw a small house
not far from the p____.
He __umped on the door
and a sweet old woman peeped out.
"What can I do for you?" she asked.

"Madam, would you like me to make you
a pot of delicious, _____ stone broth?"

"Stone _____?" asked the old woman.

My score—

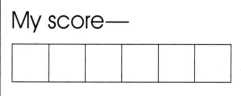

Colour in all the *th* words.

th Creative Activity Page

Draw or write the recipes for these tasty dishes.

55

The Stone in Gumtree Road

stone

smoke

roses

doze

nose

jokes

wrote

bone

home

note

rode

above

o-e Word and Sound Recognition Page

Join the sentence to the correct picture.

- The smoke is curling above the chimney.

- Water the roses, Dad.

- I'll just take a doze in the sun.

- That is a long nose, Pinocchio.

- She rode the horse over the hurdle.

- Give the dog a bone.

- There's no place like home.

- Ian wrote a note to Jenny.

On the other side

Write as many o-e words as you can. Write a sentence that has a word with o-e in it, as in stone.

o-e Read, Write and Draw Page

Wordshapes

| homework | joke | drover | clothes | froze | lonely |

Complete the word families.

joke	tone	close
p _____	al _____	h _____
st _____	c _____	p _____
br _____	dr _____	supp _____
aw _____	b _____	r _____

Yes or No
- All jokes are funny. _____
- A drover looks after cattle. _____
- A nose sits on the end of an ear. _____
- In the winter the sea is frozen over. _____
- Homework is only for big children. _____

On the other side
Write and draw a story about Pinocchio and his very l-o-n-g nose.

o-e Cloze Page

I suppose you have heard about a town
in Australia called Gumtree?

One morning, the Mayor of Gumtree
r_d_ his horse into town.
"The people of Gumtree are b_n_ lazy!" he cried.
"They have br_k_n my heart.
The town is dirty and messy. Rubbish is everywhere.
It's h_p_less!
It's time the people w_k_ up to themselves!"
The Mayor r____ back home and thought up an idea.
"I will teach them a lesson," he said.
At the stroke of midnight,
he crept out alone and placed
an enormous stone right in
the middle of Gumtree Road.
The next day some shopkeepers walked along.
"Who put this s____ on the road?" they wondered.

My score—

Colour in all the o-e words.

o-e Creative Activity Page

Draw the things you would love to find in a treasure chest — just for you.

Time to Rhyme

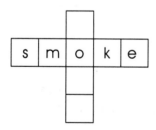

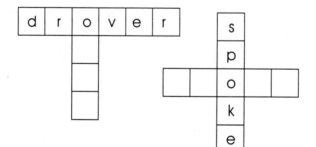

s | p | o | k | e

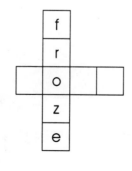

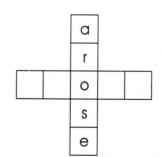

Word Bank

joke
over
bloke
stone
bone
those
doze

No Worries!

lovers

money

honey

grandmother

colour

coming

brother

done

Someone

lovely

monkey

above

⊙ Word and Sound Recognition Page

Join the sentence to the correct picture.

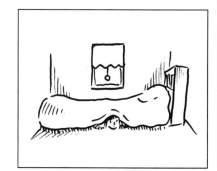

- Two lovers are kissing in the moonlight.

- Bread and honey is very yummy.

- I coloured in the lovely picture.

- My grandmother loves me.

- A wonderful star shone in the sky.

- I had three jars of money.

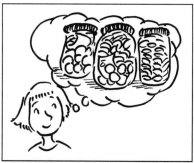

- Someone is hiding under the bed.

- I won the hopping race.

On the other side

Write as many o sounding as u words as you can. Write a sentence that has a word with an o sounding as u in it.

 62

Read, Write and Draw Page

Wordshapes

| wonderful | honey | mother | coming | love | monkey |

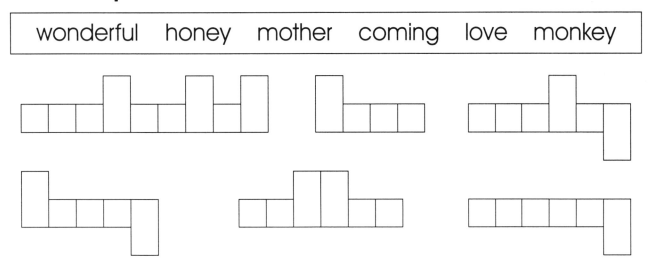

Complete the word rhymes.

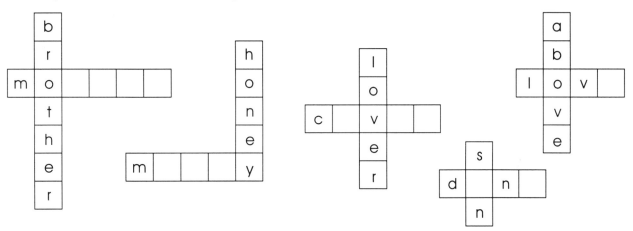

Yes or No
- Monday is the best day of the week. _____
- My mother is lovely. _____
- Somewhere over the rainbow is a big pot of gold. _____
- No one needs any money. _____
- Honey is sticky. _____

On the other side
Write and draw a story about a girl and her brother swimming in a big lake of honey.

o Cloze Page

Once upon a time,
in a small bark hut on the banks
of a lovely billabong,
there lived a tired mother
and her dreamy son.
One morning the m_____ said,
"My bones are very sore, son. I w__nder
if you'd mind going to the store
to buy me s___ butter."

"No w_____s, Mother," said the s___.
"I'll be back in the tick of a clock."
It was such a hot day that, by the
time the son had come home,
the butter had melted away to nothing.
"You silly boy!" cried the _____.

My score—

Colour in all the words with o sounding as u (e.g. mother, son, worries, some, wonder).

o Creative Activity Page

There are eight things different in picture B. Mark each one with an arrow.

Picture A

Picture B

Draw and colour in two funny scenes from the story.

Not the Three Wishes Again!

train

bait

faint

tail

snail   rain   pain

quail

wail   daily

paint

raisin

ai Word and Sound Recognition Page

Join the sentence to the correct picture.

- The train is at the station.

- The small boy fainted.

- The snail crawled onto the lettuce leaf.

- Rain, rain go away.

- Paint the fence white.

- The baby wailed for its mother.

- Use a worm for bait.

- Sam the dog wagged his tail.

On the other side

Write as many *ai* words as you can. Write a sentence that has a word with *ai* in it, as in p*ai*n.

ai Read, Write and Draw Page

Wordshapes

| against | paint | waiting | rain | explain | fail |

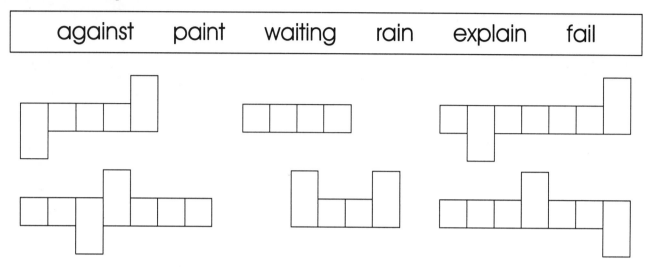

Complete the word families.

t <u>ail</u>	tr <u>ain</u>	f <u>aint</u>
p _____	r _____	p _____
f _____	gr _____	t _____
m _____	m _____	s _____
s _____	dr _____	_____

Join the word to its meaning.

- raisin   hurts a great deal
- daily   dirty mark
- sailor   a dried fruit
- raise   each day
- painful   goes to sea
- stain   to lift up

On the other side

Write and draw a story about a little boy painting a dog's tail red.

ai | Cloze Page

The wood cutter's grandson was upset.

"I'm afr _ _ d you're right," he said,

"I'm sick of hearing about it.

Again and _ _ _ _ _ _ people ask

us about Grandpa's three wishes.

They never talk about anything else.

I'm just pl _ _ _ fed up with it."

The wood cutter's grandson got ready for work.

"What time will you be home?"

asked his wife.

"At dusk once ag _ _ n," he replied f _ _ ntly.

But at morning tea time he raced home,

screeching happily.

"Gail! _ _ _ _ !"

(for that was the name of his wife)

"Gail, you'll never guess in a million years

what has just happened."

My score—

Colour in all the *ai* words.

ai Creative Activity Page

How many stories about the number THREE can you think of?
e.g. *The Three Wishes, The Three Pigs*. Draw three of your
favourites here.

The Army Lives Right Here

flight

moonlight

sunlight

fright

lightning

tight

high

right

bright

night

frightening

might

igh Word and Sound Recognition Page

Join the sentence to the correct picture.

- It's fun going on a balloon flight.

- Cats prowl in the moonlight.

- Sunlight makes things grow.

- The ghost gave him a fright.

- Lightning zipped across the dark sky.

- That lightglobe is very bright.

- These trousers are too tight.

- She is the best high jumper at school.

On the other side

Write as many *igh* words as you can. Write a sentence that has an *igh* word in it, as in m*igh*t.

igh Read, Write and Draw Page

Wordshapes

frightening	mighty	high	flight	light	sigh

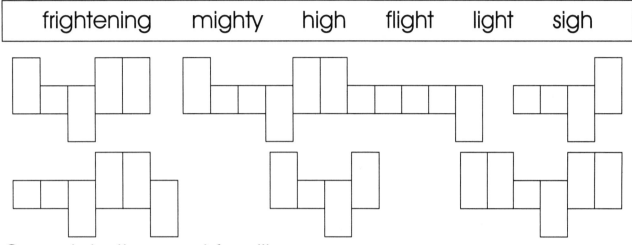

Complete the word families.

right
b _____
f _____
_____
_____

light
f _____
de _____
moon _____
s _____

ight
s _____
n _____
m _____
_____

Read and Draw

A bright night light.	A frightening sight.	A delightful flight.

On the other side

Write and draw a story about a frightening fight in the moonlight.

igh Cloze Page

Wake up!
Get out of bed!
Wash your face!
Eat your toast!
Clean your teeth!
All r_ _ _ _ _! All _ _ _ _ _ _!
Quick march!
Left! R_ _ _ _ _!
Pack your bag!
Remember your books!
Take your lunch!
Behave yourself!
Give me a kiss!
Hurry up!
Look br_ _ _ _ _! Look _ _ight!
Quick march!
Left! _ ight!
It's the same thing again
when I race to room 10:
more army commands,
more angry demands.
Hurry up! Two straight lines!
Be quiet! Sit down!

My score—

Colour in all the *igh* words.

igh Creative Activity Page

Draw some things that would happen if you could boss your Mum or Dad (or teacher!)

Draw and write three things you will *never* say to your children when you are grown-up.

I will *never* say, "_____ _____ _____	I will *never* say, "_____ _____ _____	I will *never* say, "_____ _____ _____

Mr Brown's Smelly Socks

tower

tow

crown   growl   brown   allowed   power

sow   cow   crowd   flower   town

ow Word and Sound Recognition Page

Join the sentence to the correct picture.

- Rapunzel climbed up the tower.

- The king's crown toppled off.

- A lion's growl is loud.

- A sow is a female pig.

- The brown cow sat down.

- The crowd cheered.

- A flower bloomed in the sun.

- There are skyscrapers in the town.

On the other side

Write as many *ow* words as you can. Write a sentence that has an *ow* word in it, as in brown.

Read, Write and Draw Page

Wordshapes

power	row	allowed	crown	downstairs	howl

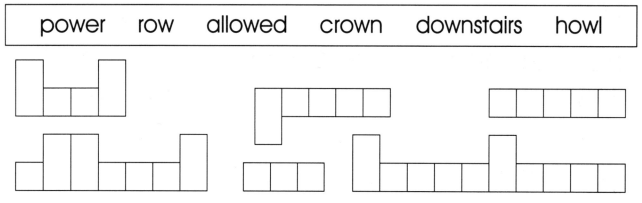

Complete the word families.

c <u>ow</u>	d <u>own</u>	<u>owl</u>
n_____	fr_____	gr_____
h_____	dr_____	j_____
w_____	br_____	h_____
s_____	cr_____	f_____

Circle the correct word.

- She is not   allowed / allow   to go.

- The crowd shouted when the king waved.   power / cow / crow

- You must come how from that tower now, Rapunzel.   bow / down

On the other side

Write and draw a story about a king and queen wearing crowns in a big crowd.

ow Cloze Page

"Get the helicopter and a frogman
with a mask, NOW!"
gr_ _led the police officer.
Mr Br_ _n was lifted _ _ _ _ _ the stairs.
A robot picked off his socks,
not a minute too soon.
(The smell bunged up its works).
The socks were put into jail,
never to be all_ _ed out again.
And what of Mr Brown?
He's wearing his gumboots again,
but never will Mrs _ _ _ _ _ _
all_ _ him to wear another
pair of socks.

My score—

Colour in all the *ow* words in brown.

OW Creative Activity Page

Draw a picture of Mr Brown's gumboots with his L-O-N-G toenails poking through the toes. Then, draw eight ways you could use some worn-out socks.